MY BRUTAL BEAST

MELISSA CUMMINS

ALSO BY MELISSA CUMMINS

DEDICATION

To anyone who's ever felt alone. You deserve to be seen, to be loved, and to have multiple orgasms.

NEVER MISS A RELEASE

To get information on works in progress, new releases, and receive exclusive discounts, giveaways, and bonus content, make sure to subscribe to my newsletter!

AUTHOR'S NOTE

Halloween is always my favorite time of year. I have a ritual, scary movies that I've watched so many times I can recite the words to and hunting for new witchy and otherworldly shows. You get the idea.

Last year I was busy writing Night Fall so I didn't have a lot of time to enjoy my normal festivities. But, I did manage to get in one Jeepers Creepers movie marathon, and that's how this book was born.

I decided that the monster in the movie had some qualifications we all love in our romance books. He's dedicated, determined, he never stops, he won't even sleep, and you can't outrun someone with wings. If you ignore the murder and mayhem he's really not that bad. So, I decided to give all of you a nice, short, spicy read with a main male character who meets all of the above.

With that being said, My Brutal Beast is intended for mature audiences. This story contains references to physical abuse and detailed depictions of emotional, mental, and sexual abuse, including sexual assault, extreme violence, murder, explicit language, sexually explicit scenes, and blood drinking.

This book also has: Dubcon and CNC scenes, depictions of manipulation, decapitation, fatphobia, kidnapping, unknown drug use, pregnancy (in epilogue), discussions of trauma, negative self-worth, unknown depression, attempted murder, alcoholism, and child abuse and neglect.

The following kinks have also been included in this work: Praise, Pleasure Dom behavior, breath play, multiple orgasms, knotting, breeding, and primal play.

PROLOGUE
CREATURE

When we were created, the earth was still young. Humans were but tiny babes, unable to grasp even a fraction of the world around them.

Our task was to protect them against those who would ruin them. There were beings on this land who would dig their talons deep into humans' tiny souls and slash away at their purity. Those voids would fill with a darkness so endless they would never recover.

We were given wings to fly great distances without obstruction, and scales and webbed hands and feet to swim through the seas. We awoke at night like statues come to life to hunt the ghosts, demons, and creatures that deserved our scorn and deliver unto them righteous retribution.

But over time we became defective.

Some of us fell in love with corrupt humans,

bedding and breeding them for our own pleasure. Some of us listened to the dark creatures, bent to their wills until we became like them. And then there were others, like me, who experienced too much war, too much strife and misery, to be anything but a demonic shell of ourselves.

The gods abandoned us.

Now I have changed the terms of my mission, of my existence. I do what I want, when I want, and how I want.

But my soul is not all black. No. There are still flickers of light, and it is those flickers that cause me to protect humans to this day. But for those who steal, rape, murder, and commit genocide? Those who believe they are the highest, smartest predator in the food chain?

Those, I hunt.

Those, I chase.

And when I catch them, I gut them like game, rip the flesh from their bones, and feast on them like the vermin they are.

CASSANDRA

My head pounds from exhaustion. I've been overworking myself, aiming for a promotion. I believed the money would make a difference in my life and I'd finally feel like I made something of myself, something more than a convict's daughter. I have to pour every inch of myself into this. So when Chelsea's name flashes across my screen, I let it go to voicemail. She was a huge party girl in college, and wherever she is, there's bound to be liquor.

But then Heather and Amy both call my cell. They take turns blowing up my phone until, with a sigh, I answer. One four-way call filled with endless pleading and a guilt trip over how I "never come out with them anymore," am "wasting my life working for a promo-tion I'll never get," and am "acting like the worst friend ever," and I agree to go out with them for dinner and drinks.

I don't tell them how much their words hurt me. That friends I've had for three-and-a-half years can't believe in me or understand how important this promotion is to me is shocking. But I ignore that hurt because maybe they are right. Maybe I haven't been available enough or checked in as often as I should have. Maybe I have been, without realizing it, a bad friend.

When I get home, I take a deep breath and promise myself I'll only be out for two or three hours. Long enough to catch up. I slip into a short pink dress that does a good job hiding just how large my stomach really is. Then I put on a pair of dark brown wedges that almost match the color of my skin and make me a couple of inches taller.

When I arrive at Wesley's and see Chelsea, Heather, and Amy, with their high-pitched squeals and easy laughs, I should be happy to see them, but I'm not. Something is wrong. I can feel it in my gut, like a sickness I don't know how to cure. And no matter how much I try to tell myself that it's me, *not* them, it won't go away.

So I plaster on a fake smile. I eat and laugh with them as if nothing is wrong, because if I'm being honest, I've been faking it for so long that it feels more natural to me than the truth.

The bill comes, and for the first time tonight, I smile genuinely. I'm ready to go.

And then it happens.

Chelsea leans forward, her blue eyes so intense she reminds me of a snake ready to strike.

"You're not getting off that easy," she says with a cold grin. The statement is meant to sound like a joke, but I can hear the threat underneath it as clear as day.

"What do you mean?" I ask.

"I know that look. You're planning on skipping out on us." Chelsea wags one perfectly manicured finger at me.

I force my spine to relax. Chelsea is very much the leader of our group, and I understand that. We all have trauma and our own ways of working through it. Hers is ordering around everyone she can, drinking, and going home with any guy who has a couple hundred dollars in his wallet. It's important for her to feel extravagant, in control, and on occasion be both judge and jury. She has no issue sharing her opinion and she can be brutal in her delivery. What's more, if Chelsea starts raining down hellfire, Heather and Amy will jump in as well.

I can't manage that, not today. I'm too tired. Whether it's from work, life, or trying to be something I'm not doesn't matter. The fact is, I don't have the backbone to protect myself. I'm walking on borrowed time already, and if one of them pushes me, I'll fold.

"Chels, you know I have an early day tomorrow," I

say in a gentle tone, then look at Heather and Amy, begging them to understand. "And I've really been struggling to keep my head above water at the firm. Maybe—"

"So you're bailing on us again? I don't know why I expected anything else from you," Amy hisses as she crosses her arms.

I haven't bailed on them that much, have I?

"Guys, I'm sorry if I haven't been around lately. I've just been working really hard for—"

"Your promotion, we know!" Heather throws her arms in the air with a loud huff. "All you talk about is your fucking promotion—"

"And we're starting to believe it means more to you than we do," Chelsea says as she settles back into her chair. The corner of her mouth curls and I realize she knows. She knows exactly what those words will do to me.

I'm instantly sent spiraling through space and time into the body of the small child who was made to feel worthless, like a burden to everyone who should have cared about her. Guilt claws at my heart. I would never want to make anyone feel like that—never want to hurt someone in the same ways I've been hurt—and my friends know that. They know I'll be too lost searching for absolution to care about my self-preservation.

The memory fades, but the pain is everlasting. My lip quivers as I push myself to speak. "I'm so sorry. I never, *ever* want any of you to feel that way."

"We know." Chels reaches her hands across the table to grasp my own.

"We know you're busy," Heather says as she rubs my arm, "but it just feels like you've forgotten about us."

"No! No, I swear I haven't." I shake my head and hold Chels' hands tighter.

"Then hang out with us tonight, okay? It's just one night, and it would really mean the world to us," Amy says, squeezing my shoulder.

I nod because for some reason I can't say the words. And if I were paying attention, I would have realized their grasps feel less like warmth and comfort and more like weighted chains tying me to them, pulling me where they want me to go.

But I don't. I don't realize it when they pile into the back of my car and direct me where to go. In fact, I understand the rationale. It makes more sense to take one car and for me to drive. That way, I can't leave them when I want to. And of course, I don't complain. I'm too busy feeling terrible that my friends know I'll want to go home long before they do. But they promise me that they'll respect my limits no matter what and we'll call it a night with enough time for me to get some sleep for tomorrow.

I still don't realize their manipulation when they laugh over large margarita glasses but don't even bother to ask if I want something as simple as water. Nor do I realize it when they call a group of guys over to our table, bat their eyelashes, and shyly stroke the men's arms and egos, until they convince them to dance—leaving me completely alone.

I've never been extroverted like they are. I prefer to keep away from large gatherings, and the rare times they've dragged me to a party, I've waited in some dark, vacant corner until they're done. It might be inconsiderate to leave me to be hounded by men and fend off people who want to take our table, but it's what I'm used to.

But when Chelsea, Heather, and Amy ask me to cover their two-hundred-dollar tab because they all "forgot" their wallets in their cars, I start to realize it. When I keep trying to call it a night only to be yelled and cursed at by my so-called friends until finally, to save the peace, I drive them to another bar, I start to realize it.

And now as I watch them dancing, their laughter spilling out around them while they tell each other drunkenly how much they love one another, I can't unsee it. I don't belong. I'm invisible to them, and I wish I could say it wasn't my fault. I wish I could blame someone else, *anyone* else, but I can't.

The reason I'm sitting at this bar is because I'm gullible, naive, and fucking *stupid*. I have spent so much of my life being those things that I don't know how to be anything else.

I've always wanted to see the good in people, to believe that there's good out there. I thought if I worked hard enough, went to college, got a job, made friends, dated, and tried to fall in love, the ache inside of me would finally go away, but it didn't.

Instead, it's grown bigger and bigger, and like a fool, I've continued to tell myself that one day the ache of loneliness will subside. That if I continue to stuff my life with what society promises will make me feel fulfilled, I'll be happy. Maybe I would be if I had picked the right people.

But they never understood me beyond how they could use me, and all this time that's what I've been feeling. That has been the horrible distension in my gut, the negative cloud that envelops me every time they call. I've stuck with them and said "yes" at every turn because I'd lost everything once, and I didn't want to be left alone again. I thought trading my comfort for their companionship—for people who wanted me when no one else did—was worth it. But it isn't.

My intuition has been screaming at me since the beginning that they don't care about me, but I was so starved for affection that I ignored it.

And I would continue to if I could. I'd live in my little bubble with my fake friends, busting my ass at a job I don't even like, surrounded by people who steal my ideas and put down my contributions. That life may be unfulfilling, but it's mine, and I know it inside and out.

But that life no longer satisfies me. I can't accept it

anymore; my exhaustion won't let me. I'm simply too tired to continue to let myself be treated this way.

Something in me has snapped. I can no longer see the world with the same rose-colored glasses. I can't simply believe that if I try a little harder, fake it a little longer, I'll eventually get to where I want to go. But I don't know what to do. I don't know where to turn.

Right now, I want to walk away from them and never look back. I can almost feel my legs moving, feel the wind in my dark curly hair. I can taste the fresh air of the parking lot and the thought of driving as fast as I can from them feels like heaven. A release to the pent up misery I've known for far too long.

But I also know it's wrong. Regardless of how upset I am with Chelsea, Heather, and Amy, they're drunk. Anyone could take advantage of them, and while I'm sure at least one of them has their cell phone, I doubt they'd be able to order an Uber by themselves. Honestly, I wouldn't be surprised if they hopped into the first car that showed up without even checking if it was their driver.

So, I'll stay. I'll temper my hurt, ignore the pitiful look from the bartender who knew I was being played from the moment we walked through the door, and use the next hour to figure out how to get through all of this. Because it isn't just about dropping my friends. It's about conquering the fear that makes me feel and fixing myself so I never let this happen again.

I don't know how long I've been scrolling through Google or how many articles I've read, but at least I feel a little more understood and not as alone.

I've learned that setting boundaries, even by just saying the word "no," can be a good first step in reclaiming my sense of self. I can't remember the last time I said the word "no" and stuck to it. In fact, it's almost impossible for me to do. It feels as if it's a right everyone else around me has, but one I was never born with.

The articles also say it can feel that way if you were often taken advantage of by a narcissist. And after a quick search of the word "narcissist," I can confirm that to be true.

Even with my low self-esteem, I know I don't deserve the things that happened to me when I was a child. My parents abused and neglected me, and I've taken enough psychology classes to know this is where all my problems stem from.

I've never gone to therapy. It was shoved into my head that I'm forbidden to talk about what happened inside of our household. Instead, I must be impeccable—well-mannered, well-dressed, never wear my natural hair, be skinny—and when I can't do that, at least act like I'm trying to lose the weight. As a kid, I had to be like all the other kids, no—I had to be *better* than all the other kids. I couldn't be a normal black girl who played outside until my sneakers were dirty. I had to be prim and proper—a princess, the belle of every ball—and represent my family to the utmost level of perfection.

But that mentality is the reason I work so hard today. And if I can see how horribly toxic it is to my psyche, then maybe it's also time to open up and share that I'm struggling.

But I can't just leave and go to a therapy appointment at 2 o'clock in the morning. Instead, I end up on Reddit, lured in by one post in the AmITheAsshole community, and decide the anonymity will be a good way for me to share my own story. The minute I hit *post,* I expect the worst, but instead I receive dozens of comments that are not only overwhelmingly positive, but from people who can relate to what I'm going through.

I've never received that type of support from

anyone. It has me pressing on the corners of my eyes to keep myself from crying.

The stool beside me squeaks loudly, rousing me from my thoughts. A handsome man with brown hair, dark brown eyes, and brown skin sits beside me. He gives me a smile of perfectly white teeth, and I can feel the charm radiating off him.

I give him a small nod and polite smile in return but focus on my drink, hoping he'll take the hint that I want to be left alone. He doesn't.

"Hi, I'm Maxton," he says, angling toward me. "Mind if I join you?"

"I'm sorry, but I'm really not in the mood tonight," I reply, not able to keep the sadness from my voice.

"I noticed. That's why I came over here." At the raise of my eyebrow, he holds up his hands, and his easy smile returns to his lips. "I didn't mean that the way it sounded. I'm the designated driver for my friend tonight, and over the last thirty minutes I've been here, you caught my eye. You are an incredibly beautiful woman. At first, I thought you were with someone, but you've been by yourself the entire time. You *have* been looking at that group of girls over there every so often, so I thought we might be in the same boat, watching our friends have fun while we're bored out of our minds."

I clasp my hands around my drink and nod. "We are in the same boat as far as that's concerned, but I really won't be great company tonight. I'm pretty down about my life and I doubt you'd want to hear about that."

Maxton leans forward, setting his arm on the counter in front of me. "Try me."

I tilt my head. He's a complete stranger, and while I doubt that his intentions are innocent and he only came over here to "talk," it would help the time go by faster until Chelsea, Heather, and Amy are ready to leave. Maybe it wouldn't be so bad to share just a bit about what's going on. The worst-case scenario is he'll get so bored with the conversation he'll leave.

"Alright." I nod over my left shoulder. "I've known those girls over there for almost four years, and tonight I finally realized we're not really friends. They call me when they need to use me for something, not because they care, and I've had enough. I'm also killing myself over a job I don't want and I'm pretty dissatisfied with my life in general."

Maxton lets out a low whistle. "Wow."

"Mmhmm, pretty depressing, huh?" I say as I wipe at the water droplets on my glass, trying to distract myself from the heaviness settling into my shoulders.

"No," Maxton says. "I think you're brave for real-izing you need to make some changes in your life. Life is meant to be fun and easy, not a constant struggle. It's way too short for that, and you deserve better."

I turn to him with a small smile, "Thank—"

"Maxton, my buddy, introduce me to your hot-ass friend!" a masculine voice says, and it's the only warning I get before a pale arm drapes across my shoulders.

"Hey! Get off!" I push the man's hand from my shoulder, but he puts it back, sliding it dangerously close to the side of my breast.

"Aww, now, honey, don't play hard to get," he slurs. His sandy blond scruff tickles my skin as he whispers, "It makes me excited."

My adrenaline spikes and I turn to defend myself from this idiotic man, but I never get the chance.

Maxton grabs the stranger's wrist and shoves his arm away from me. "Palmer, she told you to get off. Stop it!"

"Dude, what the fuck is your problem, huh?" Palmer buffs out his chest and moves to stand toe-to-toe with Maxton. "You're always on my fucking case and acting like you're better than me."

Maxton raises his hands. "Palmer, calm down. Let's just go."

"No, fuck you!" Palmer punches Maxton so hard he topples into me. My side slams against the edge of the bar, and I grab onto it to keep from falling off the stool.

Maxton recovers, but not before the bartender hits his fists against the counter. "Hey! Get the hell out of my bar!"

"Fuck—"

The bartender's eyes narrow and his voice grows cold. "I'm not going to say it again."

Palmer holds up two middle fingers, walking backward until he reaches the door and slams it behind him.

Maxton rights the stool beside me while I try to stop my heart from beating out of its chest.

"Are you okay?" I ask.

"Yeah," he says in a strained voice. "I'm sorry about that. Did I hurt you?"

I shake my head. "No, but is he always like that?"

"He can be an angry drunk, but once he's inside the car, he'll fall asleep until he gets home." Maxton opens his wallet and pulls out a twenty-dollar bill and a business card. "Look, I'd like to pay for your drink and another one if you want it." He pauses expectantly, and I realize I never gave him my name.

"Cassandra."

"Cassandra, I meant what I said earlier. You do deserve better. And if you ever need someone to talk to or you'd like to go out for dinner sometime, give me a call."

"Thank you." I take the twenty and the business card with a small nod, even though I won't call him. The moment he leaves, I drain my drink and let the cold liquid soothe me.

After a few deep breaths, I feel a little more settled and decide it's time to go. Even if Chelsea, Heather, and Amy say they don't want to leave, they can find their own way home. I've had enough of tonight. But when I move to slide off the barstool, the room begins to spin.

I grip the edge of the bar, trying to steady myself, but my head feels so foggy and heavy it's nearly impossible. The music in the bar is too loud, the people too close, the air too stifling, and I need to escape it all.

I use the bar and wall to guide myself away from the crowd, simply trying to focus on putting one foot in front of the other until I make it to the bathroom. A wave of nausea hits me, and I spin toward the toilet but manage not to throw up.

I don't understand what's happening. I haven't had any alcohol, yet I feel drunk.

The nausea subsides, and I manage to shuffle to the sink. I throw cold water on my face, but it doesn't help. Instead, when I look up to see my reflection, my vision doubles and I almost faint.

It's too hard to breathe in here. I need fresh air.

I leave the bathroom and follow the red *Exit* sign, which leads me to the back of the bar. The cool night air gives me goosebumps, but it also helps me focus. Each step I take is slow and careful so I won't fall. I remember where my car is, and if I can just make it there, I'll feel better.

I'll just take a nap, that's it. Just a little nap, and then whatever this is will pass.

"Cassie? Hey, are you okay?"

The voice startles me. It's Maxton, standing only a few feet away.

"N-no. I don't know..." Suddenly, the air feels as though it's being pulled from my lungs. The world begins to spin and my knees buckle beneath me.

Maxton wraps his arms around me, catching me before I hit the pavement.

"Car," I manage to gasp out, pointing weakly in its direction. "Help me to...my car...please."

"Alright." He adjusts his grip around my waist, supporting my weight as I try to hold onto his shoulders. "Don't worry. I've got you."

Relief surges through me as we stagger to the parking lot. But there is something else, a sense of dread that begins to prickle at the back of my neck, as if my mind is picking up on something that I can't quite understand.

I try to ignore the feeling and focus on finding my car. Seeing my blue SUV gives me a tiny ray of hope. Unable to voice the words, I muster all of my strength and point to my vehicle. My limbs continue to grow heavy until Maxton has to half-drag me against the cement, but even then, I tell myself it'll all be okay. Yet the panicked dread continues.

It's so strong it feels as though it's choking me. My heart is at odds with my body, beating faster while I move slower, and then I realize why.

Maxton is no longer dragging me to my car. We're moving sideways in another direction. It's difficult to pick up my head, but when I manage to, the sight in front of me fills my gut with terror. Palmer is standing on the passenger side of a large pickup truck, and the smirk on his face makes my blood run cold. He no longer seems drunk or belligerent, but calm and collected.

They did this to me somehow. I try to play the night back over in my mind, and it dawns on me that they must have spiked my drink.

"Hey, Cassie," Palmer says as he closes the distance between us. "Looks like you could use a little help getting home, huh?"

"Stop!" My voice is barely a whisper, but it's fueled by every ounce of strength I have left. I struggle against Maxton's grip, pushing against his body. "Let me go!"

"Easy now." Maxton snickers, tightening his hold on me. "We're just trying to help you out."

My tongue feels thick and swollen but I manage to say the words, "Y-you drugged me."

"Ah, she's smarter than she looks." Palmer chuckles and moves to grab my arm.

Adrenaline floods my system, providing me with enough strength to shove Maxton while I try to throw my body to the ground. The move forces him to lose his grip on me, and I collapse onto the gritty asphalt.

"Damn it, Maxton!" Palmer snaps.

"Stay away from me!" I cry out as loudly as I can, but it's no use. I can't move. I can't do *anything* to defend myself, and they know it. It hurts, knowing no one will save me. No one cares enough to. For whatever reason, the universe has decided I haven't suffered enough.

It isn't fair. It isn't fair!

Suddenly, a movement catches their attention. I want to turn my head to look at it, but I can't.

"Hey, buddy, move—"

There's a scream. It's a kind I've never heard before. The high shrill causes a violent shiver to run through my body. My eyes droop close, and when I open them again, I see threads of red. It almost looks like rain when it splatters over the pavement, but the tang and smell is metallic. Somewhere in the back of my mind, I know it's blood, but I don't understand why.

Someone—no, *something*—rips their bodies apart. It tears through their muscles and sinews, spilling organs and intestines out onto the cement. Their limbs are pulled off their torsos, and Maxton's head rolls close to me, his brown eyes wide and unblinking. Where two humans stood, there is now nothing but carnage and death.

The scene is gruesome, the corpses shred around me like paper. And yet, I feel calm and safe. Someone picks me up and cradles me against their warm chest. I can't make out his features, but it's a man with impossibly gray skin. Then I'm floating, and the last thing I see is the top of the bar sign before my vision fades to black.

3

CREATURE

I'm restless. It feels as though a thousand ants are crawling underneath my skin, and no matter what I do, I can't make it stop. Finally, I succumb to the one thing that has always brought me peace—soaring through the night. Yet the stretch of my wings and the brush of air against my skin do nothing to settle me. It's as if I'm being pulled toward something, and with every passing moment, it escalates. But when I see *her*, everything makes sense.

Her soul is pure light, sparkling, immaculate. In all my years, I have never seen anything like it. She is a kaleidoscope of colors, equally bright and glowing, and her darkness is just as pure. It isn't the cruel thing I've fought against for a mega-annum; it is a darkness that only serves to highlight her, to showcase her beauty even more brilliantly. And it calls to me. *She* calls to me, like the gravitational pull of the sun.

When I finally look away from the vision of her soul, I see that she is just as stunning. A mass of wild, dark brown hair cascades to her waist, perfect for me to slip my hands into when I kiss her, fuck her. Her body is a glorious thing made to be worshipped. I would get on my knees daily—no, I would *live* on them for the simple blessing of touching her, tasting between her soft thighs. I want them wrapped around my head, my hips, as I thrust into her. I want to consume her; I want her to consume *me*. The feeling of lust is so overwhelming it steals my breath.

My vantage point robs me of the ability to see more of her, something that I immediately want to rectify. But then I see them. Two men with void souls are trying to assault *my* woman. Even if I did not abide by the rules of my creator to exterminate darkness, I would still kill them. They are not fit to touch her, to be in her presence, to even gaze upon her. And for their crimes, I destroy them.

I deal with the one who touched her first—led someone so radiant, someone who should be trea-sured, into a trap—and make him scream the loudest. I rip his hand clean off and break his ribs, puncturing his lungs. He can't breathe, and that pleases me, but it isn't enough. His companion trembles in obvious shock and fear, urine running down his leg. He opens his mouth to beg, as if it might save him.

I rip their limbs from their bodies, flaying their torsos wide open. I tear at their skin, rupture their organs, and slash their heads clean off. It is over in less than two minutes, but the simmering in my blood lives on. The darkness within me begs to feast on their flesh, their bones, and I want to. I want to allow it to take me over, but my woman is lying on the filthy ground, and she deserves better.

I slip my arms under her body and cradle her to my chest. My little star is so tiny compared to me, so soft and delicate.

I'm going to keep her. It doesn't matter when or how, only that she *will* be mine. She was always meant to be mine, just as I was always meant to be hers.

I pick up her glasses, loop her bag around my neck, and take off, leaving the evidence of my retribution behind.

MY LITTLE STAR is still unconscious when we arrive home. As gently as I can, I lay her on the bed in one of the spare bedrooms. Her skin is pale, and her breathing is shallow and labored. She has several scrapes on her arms and a bruise where one of the men grabbed her. She is covered in dirt and grit, and I lift my hand and carefully run one claw over her cheek, wiping away the sediment.

My instincts scream at me to erase these reminders from her skin. But I can't do that in my original form. When I think of what I saw tonight it makes me want to roar, to obliterate something, anything—*everything*. It is what my body is built for, but right now my little star needs kindness, not my claws.

I shift into the form I use for human dealings. My grayish skin becomes pale, my claws and talons retract into human fingers and toes, my sclera turns from black to white, and my irises from luminescent white to a dark brown. But I do not hide my wings or tail from her. Truthfully, I wish to hide nothing from her, but I've seen the way my prey look at me when I hunt them. I've seen the shock and fear in their eyes, and I do not want that for my little star. I want her to never fear anything again, *especially* me.

I move to the bathroom and wet a cloth when I hear her stir. She coughs once, then again, and it is only due to my inhuman speed that I am able to grab a trash can for her before she vomits. I help her settle back into the pillows. Her brown eyes are glazed over and disoriented, likely from the chemical substance I can smell on her breath.

I move the wet cloth over her mouth and chin, cleaning her, then brush my hand across her damp forehead. "I'll be right back. I'm going to bring you some medicine."

She tries to reply, but talking seems too difficult for her. Then, she attempts to smile. The gesture falls slightly short, as she's only able to tip up one side of her mouth, but it fills me with warmth and settles me in a way I never thought possible.

I come back to her with one of the potions I was given from the members at the Central Otherworld Agency. While there are humans, witches, and every species of the Otherworld there, this potion was specifically made to heal my kind. I don't know how it will work on my little star, but I have nothing else to give her. Although I have lived around humans for a long time, I do not know much about their illnesses. But I do know I don't want her to be in pain.

I return to the bedroom where my little star rests and caress her cheek with the backs of my fingers. "I need you to open your mouth for me, little star. I have medicine that will make you feel better."

She lets out a soft moan, but her eyes remain closed. After a moment her lips part slightly. I pour the potion into her mouth, then stroke her throat with my thumb to encourage her to swallow. She instinctively does, consuming the entire vial. I try to ignore what the feeling of her throat working under my palm does to me. If I were a lesser being, a darker one, I would take her right here—near unconsciousness—and fuck her in every way I possibly could.

I shove down the need to possess her and force myself to take a deep breath. I brush her hair from her face and murmur, "Sleep, little star."

Though she doesn't open her eyes or speak, the lines of pain in her face are already starting to smooth. The change gives me a sense of relief, but I will still call the Central Otherworld Agency and ensure there will be no side effects.

Before that, I must tend to her. I fill a large bowl with warm water and grab another small towel before returning to her side. I undo her shoes, and a smile spreads across my face as I clean her small feet. She's a tiny thing, something that should be cared for and protected—a role I plan to fill from here on out. As I wash her calves and slowly travel up her legs, I let my mind wander. I *have* to. Touching her like this is my own twisted realm of heaven and hell, and I must stay strong and curb my desire—at least until she wakes.

It occurs to me that she may have someone out there looking after her, someone she might care for in the way I want her to care for me. The thought makes me clench the towel in my hand—not just at the possibility someone may already have my little star's heart, but that they failed her tonight. *I* almost failed her tonight. Someone should have been with her. She should have never been alone.

No, I decide. *If someone was with her at that bar and left her to fend for herself, they don't deserve to be in her life. In fact*—I snarl, baring my teeth at the thought—*they don't deserve to share the same air she breathes, to breathe at all.*

Yes, if she tells me that is the case, I will gut that spineless fuck, disembowel them, and batter them until nothing is left. All in her honor, all for her.

My little star stirs slightly as I wipe the damp cloth

along her upper thigh, my fingers grazing the hem of her gown. I hum to her, both in satisfaction of her nearness and my vengeance. Then I swallow hard at what will come next.

My heartbeat begins to race. I slowly roll her gown up, and she moves again and moans softly. I pause, not wanting to wake her. I want this chance to disrobe her, to clean her, to take care of her, and I know it could scare or anger her. I don't want that, and I don't want to stop touching her.

She settles, and I continue to raise her dress, letting my eyes trail over her skin. I take in every blemish, every mole, the stretch marks on her stomach, thighs, and hips. All of it is beautiful to me. I want to taste her everywhere. To lick her from top to bottom, feel the heat of her skin against mine. I want her to wrap her arms around me and welcome me into her body, mind, heart, and soul. It is selfish of me to want to bond with her that deeply when I'm tarnished with my own darkness, but I can't stop the desire. I can't let her go—I won't.

Soon her dress is off, and I'm left in awe of her perfection. I run my finger over her arm and watch the small goosebumps that appear. The temptation she's woken inside of me is too great, and I have to get away from her now, while I still *can*. Quickly I dress her in one of my shirts, cover her in a blanket, and then dash out of the bedroom.

I run, flying through the hallway until I am in

another wing, one where I can't hear her heartbeat or still smell her natural fragrance. But she haunts me all the same. I shove the window open and take a deep breath of fresh air, using each one to expel my need for the woman now in my home. The coolness of the night begins to calm my hot skin, and little by little I start to feel more in control.

Once I'm able to focus, I call the Central Otherworld Agency to make sure my little star will be alright. Each ring makes the nerves in my body jumble, spilling and running into one another like marbles until it feels like I can't breathe. But by the second ring Daniella answers.

"You need to give me a name so I can stop calling you Creature 0205," she says.

Her candor relieves some of my tension. Upon joining the Agency, each being receives a dedicated sponsor for a period of time. Daniella Novak, one of the founders of the Agency, is mine.

She may be right. After all, I do not know my little star's name, and I do not truly have one to give her. The Agency assigned me a fake name, but to share that with my little star seems wrong. I want things to be real between us, not filled with lies.

I turn the thought over in my head. "Is it really that important?"

She huffs a laugh. "If you want proper identification, then yes. Eventually, someone's going to question if John Smith is a fake name." Her voice softens. "It's also important if you want to make it in this world, not with other people, but with yourself. Your name is your identity. You have the ability to claim it, own it. There's power in that."

I pause at the pride in her voice. "I'll come up with one."

"Thank you. Now, why did you call me?"

"Can the healing potion you gave me be used on humans?"

"Technically, yes. For humans it would just act as a general healing tonic. Why do you ask?"

"I have a woman here—"

Her voice drops an octave as she speaks and I narrow my eyes. "What do you mean you *have* a woman?"

"She was being assaulted by two beings outside of a bar. I dealt with them and brought her back here. She was pale, fading in and out of consciousness from some sort of drug in her system. I believe they gave it to her. She threw up and I treated her with the potion afterward." I repeat the details to her in a level tone and do my best to control the way my hand shakes with the need to strike out at something.

Daniella huffs and begins typing. "What's the name of the bar?"

The question throws me off guard. "Loe's, why?"

"Because, by 'dealt with' I assume you mean killed, and you have a habit of not always getting rid of the evidence. We'll have someone take care of it." A door opens and shuts in the background. "As for your human, based on what you've told me, the potion will be fine for her. She will just need some time to let it circulate through her system, since humans heal slower than we do."

My heart skips at the news, and for once I feel... light, as if I could fly easily without my wings, without the force of gravity holding me down.

"Has she seen you in your normal form?"

"An in-between version, yes."

She hums again. "And what are you planning to tell her? Are you going to explain what happened, drop her off here?"

My tone drops to a low growl. "I'm keeping her here."

Daniella sighs. "You can't just take a human woman against her will and keep her."

"She's mine and you will *not* take her from me!" The roar that leaves me is immediate and instinctual.

But the next voice I hear isn't Daniella's. It's a masculine one even colder than my own: "Correct your tone when you're speaking to my wife, *creature*, or I will correct it for you," Gregori says.

My natural response to his threat is to rise to the challenge. To battle Gregori, Daniella, or *anyone* who would try to take my little star from me. But then I hear Daniella whisper that she's okay, and I realize he and I are the same.

My little star may not be my wife yet, but I already

feel the need to protect her and stand by her side. I want her past the flow of time. In any year, dimension, or realm, I would want her, and I've spent a little less than a few hours in her company. How would I feel if I had spent years with her? Had children with her?

The thought warms me, just as my gut clenches. I disrespected the only person who has done nothing but assist me from the moment we met. I've not been friendly to Daniella. In truth, I haven't really known how, and yet didn't she answer my call? Didn't she send people to clean up my kills? I dishonored her and in turn her husband. I owe them both more than that.

I clear my throat. "I apologize. I shouldn't have spoken to you like that." The words feel strange to me, as I've never spoken them before.

Daniella sighs. "It's alright. I know all of this is new for you. But for humans, choice and freedom are very important, and if you take those away from her, the two of you may never create the relationship you're hoping for."

The thought of losing my little star cuts through me. I've never felt this feeling, and as I look at my face in the windowpane and see how pale my skin is, and the vacancy in my eyes, I suddenly know what it is. It's fear. The same fear that I've put into the faces of so many is staring right back at me at the simple thought of losing someone I barely even know.

"You're right," I say, unable to keep the tremble out of my voice. "I...I've never felt the emotions I feel right now. I don't even know what they mean. But I just know that she feels like she's...mine."

There's a smile in her voice when she says, "Finding your mate is one of the most complex, overwhelming, and beautiful feelings you'll ever have. Congratulations on finally finding yours."

My eyes open so wide I'm surprised they don't fall out of my head. "I...did?"

I've heard the term before, but I never could have imagined that I might have a mate somewhere out there. When my species was created, we were always alone. *Always.*

There is a part of me that cares about my siblings. But we all went our own ways or fell to the darkness of this world. Some even slept, forgotten by space and time, and are nothing more than marble statues now.

I often wonder why I can't submit myself to the same fate. Why, regardless of the turbulence that lies inside of my soul, I continue to walk among the living. Perhaps, some part of me somehow knew this day would come.

"You deserve this, you know." The warmth in Daniella's tone blankets me, soothing away some of my shock. "I can't imagine what you've gone through for so many years, but you have a chance to be happy, and I hope that you will take it. Be vulnerable with her, gentle with her. Get to know her and share yourself with her. Let her see you, the real you, not the cold, detached facade you display to everyone else. If you need any help or guidance, I'm only a phone call away, okay?"

I nod, unfamiliar with the lightness in my chest. "Thank you," I whisper.

"Always," she says.

We hang up the phone and I ponder her words. I know nothing about my little star, and that is a problem I need to fix. I take a deep breath, settle into my purpose, and fly back to her wing. She's sleeping peacefully when I open the door, her dark brown curls spread out on the pillow around her. My heartbeat races simply from seeing her.

I take her dress and purse with me into the study beside her bedroom. Her dress holds no pockets, but I make a note of the brand name to order more clothing for her. Next I dump the contents of her purse onto the desk. There isn't much there—two different shades of lipstick, a lip gloss, wallet, phone, keys, and a granola bar. I pick up the wallet and read her driver's license.

Cassandra Brielle Leon.

Finally, I know something about her.

Knowing her name makes me feel as if I've obtained a small victory, and it's the key I need to learn more about her. I use my computer to run a quick background check on her using her name, birthday, and address. In minutes, I have the name of where she works, her social media profiles, and that she has two overdue romance novels at the local library.

There aren't many photos of her on her social

media profiles—mostly work functions, a few where she appears to be in the background of a large party. She looks younger there, and I figure this must have been a few years ago, possibly when she was at college.

But the one thing that comes across in each photo is that she never looks happy or comfortable. There's something missing when she smiles, and her eyes call out to me. It's as if she's been alone for just as long as I have.

You'll never be alone again.

The thought is a promise, a sacred vow. Even if she wishes to leave, I will be with her. I'll follow her, stalk her anywhere she goes, and keep trying to win her heart. There is no other option.

I click onto the most recent post she's made online, something on Reddit. Reading it, I find out *exactly* how my little star ended up at that bar tonight, and that her horrible, manipulative friends left her alone, only bothering to speak to her when they wanted her to take them somewhere else.

From her words and the comments, it's clear this has happened before. Whether it's her friends or others, it appears she has been taken advantage of and mistreated regularly. I think back to her eyes in the pictures, to the way she hid in large groups of people, and clench my fists.

She should be a queen, with the world bending to her will, and I will be the one to give that to her. She's worthy of that and so much more. I will be her loyal subject, and when she chooses me to be, her king.

But I see now that everything Daniella said is correct. My little star will need her freedom. Even if it's something she struggles to realize she should have, she will need it. She won't be able to trust me or love me without it. I cannot force her to stay here against her will. As much as I want her by my side, she must make that choice on her own.

I will do whatever I can to not only earn that trust, but show her the goodness she deserves, the care and love, the way she should be valued and treated like the goddess she is. I will do everything possible to convince her that we belong together while still allowing her the choice, no matter what she may choose.

She will never feel used or uncared for again. I will put her needs first and make her happiness my singular purpose. She is my mate, and I intend to cherish her in a way no one else ever has.

With that, I send an email to Fallon, my personal shopper. I include the pictures of Cassandra from her social media profiles, a picture of her dress, the brand name, size, and I also take measurements of its neckline, arms, shoulders, bust, waist, and chest. I include the brand name of the makeup I found in her purse and photos of her purse and wallet as well. I explain to Fallon that Cassandra is on the shorter side, perhaps around five feet. I also tell Fallon to get her any toiletries she may need in every popular scent available and anything I may have left out.

Within five minutes, Fallon responds to my email and asks if there's any budget she needs to adhere to and how many days of clothing Cassandra will need. I tell her there is no budget, and decide on a month, with a note that once Fallon meets Cassandra, she can learn more about her personal preferences and create a full wardrobe from there.

I make my way to the kitchen and take stock of the fridge and pantry. I'll need to order plenty of food to make sure my little star has everything she might want when she wakes up. I place a large delivery order from my favorite bakery—muffins, croissants, danishes, bagels, and different kinds of breads. I also get produce, vegetables, cheeses, and other dairy items sent over from the farmers' market. At the butcher shop, I order several pounds of chicken, beef, pork, and fish. And from the supermarket, I make sure to get eggs, milk, yogurt, cereal, chocolate, snacks, condiments—one of everything I can find.

The deliveries will be here first thing in the morning, and once I'm sure of my little star's favorites, I'll keep them on hand for her. I'm so busy trying to make sure I've covered everything she may need that I don't hear her. But I do sense a change in the air, the freshness of her scent and the purity of her soul and aura. My eyes lock onto her form in the doorway and I lose my breath.

For a moment, I'm stunned speechless. She looks far too vulnerable standing there in only my shirt, which falls down to her ankles like a dress, her beautiful curls spilling over her shoulders. I'm hit with the want, the *need* to make her mine, and I have to swallow to soothe the dryness in my throat.

"You're awake," I finally manage to say.

She gives a small nod and takes a single step forward.

I move closer, looking for any signs of lingering pain or disorientation. "Are you feeling alright?"

Again she nods, but her eyes are still slightly glazed, her movements somewhat languid. I don't believe the drugs have fully left her system yet.

"Let's get you back to bed," I suggest. I intend to pick her up and take her back to the bedroom, but then she does the most surprising thing: With a soft smile, she lifts the hem of the shirt up and off.

I freeze, utterly transfixed by the expanse of warm brown skin revealed to me. Every honorable intention flees my mind, replaced only by the urge to touch, taste, and claim what she's offering. It takes every ounce of restraint I possess not to give in to the desire.

"What are you doing?" I rasp.

She sways slightly on her feet. "Want you," she murmurs.

"You don't know what you're asking for, my little star," I grit out, and steady her.

As I reach for the shirt on the ground, she clasps my face. "No."

"Cassandra," I whisper, begging her to take pity on me.

She pouts. "That's not fair. You know my name, but I don't know yours," she slurs.

"Give me one, my little star." I meet her eyes, and my control begins to slip away.

She tilts her head to the side. Then she looks me over, her gaze roaming from the top of my head, to my wings, to my feet. When she meets my eyes again, there's no fear, no concern, only the same desire I feel within myself.

"Raven," she whispers.

I run the pad of my thumb over her jaw, her cheek, tucking the strands of her hair behind her ear.

"Then that will be my name," I say.

She graces me with her own smile, stepping closer, until she's flush against me. Every hair on my body stands straight, and my cock is harder than it has ever been in my entire life.

"Raven," she says again, as if she's rolling the name around in her mouth, tasting it, savoring it. Then she reaches for me, grasps my shoulders, and whispers, "I want you."

And before I can stop myself, I slam my mouth against hers.

4

———

RAVEN

The moment our lips meet, I know this is where I belong, and if I had to wait an eternity before I could experience her lips again, I would. I have seen humans kiss and fuck one another, but I never knew it could feel like this, and it never would with anyone else. My entire body tightens with need.

I'm desperate to sink into her, to rut her like the animal I am, but I focus on her pleasure. I want to devour her, drink her in, taste her, tease her, fuck her into oblivion. The heat of her lips and body brands me, and I welcome it. I need it and I'll never let her go.

I can still taste the remnants of the drug on her lips, but I don't care. She gave me permission, begged me to please her, and I'll be damned if I stop. I will never, ever stop.

Even though this is my first kiss, we immediately

fall into a rhythm. I take control of the kiss, tilting her head to the side so I can kiss her more passionately. When she opens her mouth and moans, I lick the seam of her lips, then delve inside to taste her tongue. As I rub my tongue against hers, the sensation sends shivers down my spine.

Each breath she takes makes her breasts rub against me, and I want to squeeze them, lick her dark nipples. I want to bite her, imprint my fangs all over her delectable body. The beast inside me demands I claim her.

I slide my hands down her back, gripping her ass, and pick her up. She wraps her legs around my waist and I pin her against the wall. I bite her lips, suck and pull them into my mouth. She moans, moving her hips against me, and I growl at how eager she is. She needs me just as much as I need her.

I slide my hands down her body while she holds onto my shoulders. Her skin is so soft, so perfect. I pull away from her lips to taste her. I bite the side of her jaw, trace my tongue over her ear, lick and suck down her throat, biting where her pulse pounds beneath her skin. The way she moans makes me even harder.

I cup her breasts in my hands and marvel at how perfectly they fill them. Her nipples are so hard. They beckon me, and I can't resist sucking one of them into my mouth. Her head falls back as she moans my name, and I experience a new type of nirvana.

I want more of her, to taste her more deeply, to

keep pulling those sounds of pleasure from her lips. They satisfy me as nothing else can. I'm addicted to the way she says my name. How loud can she become? How wild? What will she look like when she breaks apart for me? And she will break. I won't stop until she does.

I push my knee between her legs to hold her still as I pull and pinch her nipple with my teeth. She cries out when I brush against her clit, and I smile in satisfaction. I let her breast go with a pop and watch her, completely transfixed as she grinds against me, seeking her release.

I grab her hair at the base of her scalp and pull. Her eyes open wide, just as her moans continue to fall from her lips, faster, louder.

"Is this what you want, little star? Is grinding against my knee enough to make you come?"

"Raven." She closes her eyes, trying to hide from me, but her hips keep moving as if she's lost to this, to me, and it's intoxicating.

I grab one of her legs and spread her open, making her settle more on my knee. I rub against her clit, circling the nub, and she cries out again.

"That's it my little star, use me. Take your pleasure," I growl as she moves faster. I push against her harder. "You're so wet for me."

She clings to me, squeezing my shoulders. Her moans become louder, higher, a song of praise that I need, that I *demand* from her. "Come for me."

I bend down and suck her nipple into my mouth once more, and she hugs my head to her chest. "Don't stop, please, *please,*" she begs, as if I could even if I wanted to. I love her like this, desperate and needy for me, for only what *I* can give her.

I wrap my tail around her leg, hoisting it into the air, keeping her spread. I grasp and knead her ass, forcing her to grind faster, harder against my knee. My cock is heavy, pre-come leaking down my leg as she brushes the head with her thigh.

Then she breaks apart. Watching her come is one of the most beautiful, glorious things I've ever seen. Her face falls apart in ecstasy. She pulls hard on my hair, and it only heightens my pleasure. Her hips spasm, jerking against me as her back arches. She looks as if she's frozen, suspended in time. If I was an artist, I would capture this vision of her.

I need to see it again. I need some part of me to be inside her, to stretch her, ready her for my cock.

I give her just a moment to come down from her high, then I slide my fingers over her pussy lips. She shudders against me and I grin, my lips brushing her ear as I whisper, "How many of my fingers can you take, my little star?"

Then I slip one digit inside of her.

She jerks against me, and I use my thumb to circle her clit. Her cries urge me on. I pull her thigh higher, so I can watch the way her pussy lips close around me.

Then I lengthen my tail, glide the ribbed end over her clit and make it vibrate against her.

She shatters. She's panting, gasping, clinging, and squeezing every part of me she can. She can't speak. She only screams her pleasure, and the sound echoes through the room.

She comes again before weakly trying to push me away. For that I punish her by adding another finger and curling it in her pussy. I know I've found the spot I'm looking for when her eyes widen and she comes once more.

My hand is soaked in her juices, and I'd have it no other way. Tears fall from her eyes on her fifth orgasm. Her thighs are covered in her wetness, her body damp with sweat, and I can't wait any longer, but I need to move her to a bed. I won't be gentle when I take her, but I want her as comfortable as possible.

I wrap my arm securely around her waist, spread my wings, and fly to the bedroom. I lay my little star gently on the soft sheets. I've made her come so many times she can barely move. Her entire body is relaxed, and even though her eyes are halfway closed, she watches me with anticipation.

I shed my pants and stand before her, completely naked. Her gaze roams over me, taking me in, and she bites her lip. But when she sees my long, hard cock, her eyes widen.

"Don't worry," I say with a snarl as I pull her by her ankles, spreading her legs wide. "I'll fit." She was made for me, and I won't stop until her pretty pussy takes me all the way to the base.

I settle in between her legs and lean over her. For a moment I just stare at her, and with each second that passes by, the tension between us grows. She licks her lips and I kiss her. I lick, suck, bite, and nibble her mouth and tongue. Then I position myself at her entrance. Gods how I want to ram into her in one full thrust, but I can't—not yet.

I brush my cock against her pussy lips. I squeeze the head hard so I won't come the second I get inside of her, and then I thrust forward. We both gasp at the sensation. I shudder, try to draw in a breath as I give her inch after inch. My little star arches her back. She lifts her hips and wraps her arms around me, trying to pull me closer.

Her pussy grips me like a glove, and all the blood in my body rushes to my cock. I never imagined anything could be so powerful and potent. I would wage wars, burn the world to ash, and sacrifice my life all to have her like this. She is my Helen of Troy, my weakness and salvation.

I grip the sheets beneath me. I want to let my claws extend, to rip into the bed and fuck her with brutal intensity, but I can't. My little star is human, and the thought of hurting her is unbearable to me.

For a second I don't move; I need to adjust to her just as much as she does to me. The only sounds in the room are our pants. As I stare into her dark brown eyes, so dilated they're almost black, I whisper the one thing I know to be true: "You're mine now, forever." Then I pull out to the tip—and ram back inside.

She cries out, and it's a symphony to my ears. She digs her fingers into my back, and the bite of pain only makes me move harder, faster. I want to feel her come undone around my cock. I want to fuck her until she's delirious, until nothing matters in this world beyond us, because she's all I see.

I memorize every expression, the way she squeezes her eyes tight as tears of pleasure pour from them, the way her breasts bounce in sync with my thrust, the beautiful curve of her stomach, how she has to fight for every breath.

Her hands slip lower to the base of my wings. She squeezes, holding onto them for dear life, and the sensation that flows through me is indescribable. It turns me wild. My wings expand around us. My hips jerk uncontrollably, and her moans grow louder until she's screaming with every thrust.

I struggle to regain control. The only thing that pulls me from my madness is the thought that if I continue, I may actually break her. I grab ahold of her arms to pull her hands off me, but she only holds on tighter.

"Stop fighting me, little star," I growl.

She whimpers, and I realize she enjoys me this way, crazy and feral for her.

The noise that leaves my throat is primal. I grab

both her wrists and pin them above her head. "Hold onto the headboard."

But my little star doesn't move. Instead, she tries to pull her hands back. She rolls her hips beneath me, and I can't help the moan that slips from my lips.

I wrap my hand around her neck and squeeze. "Don't defy me, little star."

Her eyes grow wide, and the sound she makes would bring me to my knees if I weren't already on them. I wrap my tail around her wrists, keeping them pinned above her, and she finally grabs onto the headboard. Then I pull her leg over my shoulder and thrust into her harder, deeper.

The sound of the headboard slamming against the wall joins our moans and cries. With each breath I inhale the smell of our sweat and her come, and the way her pussy grips me nearly drives me insane. She's so wet, so tight, sucking me in with every thrust, covering me in her sweet juices.

She suddenly freezes. Her hips jerk, her pussy spasms around me, and she comes.

But this time it's different. This time I get to feel her release around my cock.

"Cassandra," I moan. "I'm going to breed you."

I can't get enough of her. Her release is magnificent, and I desperately want to come inside of her, give her my knot, but I need her to come one more time.

I tell myself that'll be enough because she's waning. When she comes again, I can't hold back. A jolt shoots down my spine, my body tenses, my hips move of their own volition, and I release my knot inside of her. It locks us into place. I keep filling her, more and more. My orgasm is endless, and I have enough mind to let go of her wrists and vibrate my tail on her clit once more.

Her hands struggle to grip the headboard, the sheets, anything—she's tugging the bedding off the mattress, writhing, jerking as I keep coming inside of her, and then she comes again and doesn't stop. It's as if her body is trying to compete with mine. The mixture of our come runs out of her, down our legs, leaving a puddle on the sheets. And when I pull her close and roll onto my back, she's fast asleep.

I LAY with her for hours. I should sleep, but there's a part of me that wonders if all of this is real. If when I open my eyes again, my little star will still be there.

My fear is irrational, yet it isn't until the sun comes up that it finally begins to dissipate. I rise, slowly and carefully, as to not wake up my goddess. I wet a towel and clean her legs and pussy, then tuck her in under the sheets. I have just enough time to take a shower before the deliveries start to arrive.

I put everything away and move Cassandra's wardrobe into my room in the east wing, where she will be staying. Then I call Daniella and inform her of my new name, Raven Leon. And even after all of that, my little star is still asleep.

Her long curls are splayed around her. She's on her side, snuggled to the spot I was in only a few hours prior, but she's pulled down the bedsheet. Her breasts, stomach, and one delectably curvy thigh are completely uncovered. I'm suddenly famished, and it's a hunger for something far more delicious than food.

I'm on my back, my legs spread wide around Raven's head. His tongue flicks my clit before diving in between my pussy lips once more. My hips come off the bed as he eats me like a starving man, like a *beast*. I hold onto his head—gripping his long hair in my hands—moving him exactly where I want him. He follows so obediently. He's so eager to please me, and it sends another surge of wetness down to my core.

The dream is hot and erotic, but when my back arches and I cry out, I realize it isn't a dream at all. I gasp and look down. Raven's dark brown eyes meet mine. His broad shoulders support my legs, and now that I'm awake, he feasts.

I can't think straight as he thrusts his tongue in and out of my pussy, his nose brushing against my clit. He inhales, smelling me, and I blush, but my scent only makes him want me more.

He's savage with me. I'm still so sensitive from last night that I come quickly. He growls at the taste, slides his hands under my hips to spread me open even wider, and gets back to work. I don't know how many times he makes me come, but when he kneels between my legs, I'm ready for him.

I remember everything that happened last night. Raven was there. He saved me, and while I didn't get a good look at what killed the men who drugged me, Raven is the most likely culprit.

He's not human, at least not completely. And if I hadn't been roofied, I wouldn't have asked Raven to fuck me.

But when he leans down to kiss me, I meet him halfway. I wrap my arms around him and welcome him into my body when he thrusts inside of me. He stretches me in a way that nothing and no one could ever compare to, and I'm not afraid or disgusted by him. Instead, he feels like a missing piece of me, my sanctuary, my home, and I will never get enough of him.

Our tongues twine together as he continues to pound inside of me. I moan his name, scratching my nails down his back, and he hisses.

"You're perfect," he moans. He thrusts harder, faster. The headboard hits the wall so hard I wonder if it'll break, if he'll destroy it and me. And so help me, I'd let him. I'd beg him to.

Raven leans down and bites my earlobe. I hold him close, tangle my fingers in his long hair, and cross my legs behind his back.

"I will follow you wherever you go, little star." *Thrust.* "Anywhere." *Thrust.* "Everywhere." *Thrust.* "You own me, Cassandra."

His fangs brush against my neck. "I am yours, and you, little star, are *completely* mine."

"Yes," I choke out. I don't need to question what he's saying before I respond because it's the truth. No one will ever replace him. No one can ever take the places he's claimed in me.

It could be because he's saved and took care of me, but no matter how irrational it may be, my heart is no longer my own. It belongs to him.

He growls, the sound vibrating against my neck. "Good fucking girl," he says, and then he bites me, and I scream. His fangs slide into my neck. He drinks my blood, and something there burns. But the pain is delicious, and it affects us both.

Raven grabs hold of the headboard and fucks me so hard it breaks. He puts one hand on the wall above my head and keeps going. Nothing stops him—it's as if he's possessed, and so am I. I keep crying out his name over and over and over. I tangle myself around him, breathe in the earthy scent of his sweat.

Raven is so big, maybe three feet taller than me. His body large and muscular. And even though I'm so much smaller than him, I want his full weight. I want to bask in him. He could suffocate me and I'd thank him for it.

I do everything I can to pull him closer, and he wraps his arms around me. His skin is fully pressed against mine, his dark eyes so dilated they're almost black. My arms prickle as his hair cascades around me, and his soft, leathery wings shroud us in darkness. All of it, combined with his cock filling me, takes me over the edge.

I come, screaming his name, giving him my entire body and everything that I am on a silver platter. He joins me there, and when I feel his cock expand and his hot come spill inside of me, I come all over again.

My mind is quiet. The only sound in the room is our breathing. I feel sated, relaxed. I should move my arms from around him but I simply can't. The earthy scent of him fills my nostrils, and all I want to do is get closer. It should terrify me just how much I don't want to let Raven go, but it doesn't. For the first time in my life, I feel at peace.

Eventually, he slips off the bed, and I miss his warmth immediately. But a moment later, he picks me up.

I squeal. "What are you doing?"

"I thought you might be sore." There's no arrogance in his voice, only a tenderness that softens his sharp face as he stares down at me. "I'm going to take care of you."

My face heats, both from the memory of how hard and rough he was inside of me, and also because he's carrying me. I've never been carried, not even as a little girl. I've always been too big, too overweight, and my reaction is instantaneous: "It's okay. You don't have to do that. I'm too heavy for you like this. Put me down."

Raven's eyes narrow at my words, but he drops a kiss on my forehead. "You are not too heavy for me. I'm sorry you have been surrounded by nothing but weak men who didn't care about you—much less deserve you—but they are your past, not your present or future. That role belongs to *me*. Nothing they said was true. Do not do yourself the dishonor of believing their lies."

His sincerity shocks me, and I don't know how to respond to him. He sets me down on a chair, and I hear the steady stream of water pouring from his bathtub. The world fades away as his words settle inside of me. I meet my own gaze in the mirror and take a long, hard look at myself.

My face is too plump; my neck too wide compared to my shoulders. The fat on my arms jiggles if I move too fast. My breasts, too large, rest on top of my protruding stomach, and my thighs swallow the chair, hanging over its sides.

Most of the words that come to mind when I see myself are negative. That I'm fat, big, overweight, obese, unattractive, unhealthy. That I'll get diabetes. That I'm hurting myself by not exercising more or sticking to a diet of SlimFast and salads. That I should be happy with any male attention I receive, because I'm nothing more than an easy lay.

But Raven doesn't see me that way. I can't remember the last time anyone took care of me or was a tenth as caring as Raven has been over the last twenty-four hours.

"Do you have a favorite scent?" Raven asks, pulling me from my thoughts.

He's piled the silver marble countertop with at least fifteen different bottles of bubble bath soap, and he's still gathering more items from a linen closet.

"I also have these. Fallon says you'd like them, but I apologize. I don't quite know what they are." He rolls two individual packages of bath bombs in his hands with a confused look on his face.

The balls, the bathtub, the fact that we're still naked—even how adorable he is when he's confused—fades away at the sound of another woman's name falling from his lips. White hot jealousy rushes to the surface, and I can't stop myself before I say, "Who is *Fallon?*"

At the change in my tone, he turns and immediately comes to me. He cups my face, his hands gentle as they caress my cheeks. But I'm still vibrating with anger, hurt, and a betrayal I shouldn't feel.

I barely know this man. I have no claim to him. But my body and heart won't acknowledge that.

"Fallon is my personal shopper, as I rarely leave this castle. I asked her to help me get things for you, because I wanted to make sure you would have everything you could possibly need."

Just like that, my jealousy leaves me, and I'm embarrassed. I tilt my head away from his searching gaze, and he pulls me back. I grasp his forearms and drop my head forward, but he simply squats down to my level.

"I don't know what's happening," he says, and his sincerity brings tears to my eyes. "I don't know much about human emotions, but I know I've upset you. What did I do? How can I fix this?"

I shake my head, moving to wipe my eyes, but he catches my hand and brushes my tears away.

"Please talk to me, my little star," he pleads.

"I'm sorry," I whisper. "When you mentioned Fallon, I just...got jealous that you were talking about another woman, that she bought you things and you had them here. I...I got scared—" *That you might be with someone else.* I can't bear to say that thought out loud or deal with the feelings of heartache it raises within me. "I shouldn't have felt that way, I—"

Raven tilts my chin up gently, his dark eyes staring

into my own like he can see into my soul. "You have every right to feel the way you do, my little star. In fact, I won't lie and say that a little piece of me isn't pleased. I, too, wondered if you might have someone you cared for, and got *jealous*." The way he says the word is almost like he's tasting it, trying it on, figuring out if it fits just right.

My face heats. I know I don't have to tell him. I know that life isn't this simple. I can't just meet someone and fall in love with them, and yet, I still want him to know. I *need* him to know. "There isn't anyone."

He beams. It's as if light covers every inch of his face. His smile kicks my heart into fifth gear as his tail gently thumps against my foot in pure joy. Raven wraps his arms around me and kisses me like I am all the stars, the planets, and the moons in our galaxy. Then he says, "There has never been another woman for me. Only you."

My eyes widen in surprise. "What? Never?"

"Never. You were my first. I had never even kissed a woman before or been with anyone until tonight."

I'm stunned into silence. The way Raven kissed and touched me, I was sure he had experience. Knowing this wonderful, beautiful man was a virgin, and that he not only gave me that gift, but the most orgasms I've ever had in my life, is astounding.

Raven moves to turn off the bath water, but his movements are slightly awkward.

Is he shy?

"Would you still like to take a bath?" he asks.

I nod, and though I have so many questions, I don't want to make him uncomfortable.

"Good," he says, then goes back to the counter, retrieving the line of bottles and bath bombs. Anything that doesn't fit in his arms, he carries with his tail, and I have to stop myself from chuckling at how cute he looks. "Now, which one of these would you like to use?"

"You didn't have to go through all of this trouble for me. Anything is fine, really."

His face grows serious. "No, I never want you to settle for less than you deserve—not for anything ever again. I want to know what you want and what you need, and whatever that is, I will provide it for you. I want you to feel comfortable here, with me."

I bite my lip to stop the words that almost fall out of my mouth. *I'm not worth all of this. I'm not used to this,* my mind shouts. A bubble bath is a simple thing, and yet he looks at me as if my choice is more important than his next breath.

"Tell me what you want, my little star, and I will move the heavens and the earth to get it for you." His voice is captivating, seductive, pulling at my long-awaited desire, my hope that someone would finally just want me. That I would be enough, that my happiness would finally matter.

It's a lull I can't resist, and finally I whisper, "Flowers. I like the smell of flowers."

He smiles, and the pleasure on his face makes my heart pound.

Raven carefully places everything down and picks out two bottles. "These are floral scents. Which one do you like?"

I smell the first one. It reminds me of a summer garden: fresh roses, daisies, and a warm breeze. The second one is completely different, with lavender, vanilla, and jasmine. The moment I inhale it, my entire body relaxes. "This one."

Raven purrs, and the vibration soothes me more than the scent of the soap. He pours it into the bath along with some Epsom salt, then presses a button and starts the Jacuzzi. In seconds the bathtub is filled with bubbles, and the fragrant scent begins to fill the bathroom. I let out a soft sigh.

Raven sets to putting the other bath soaps away. I move to help him, but he stops me with a kiss. My heart swells at the action, at how he clearly cares for me, but it also confuses me.

This is all so new, moving too fast, and a small part of me wonders if I've lost my mind, while the rest of me simply wishes to bask in these feelings. I can't reconcile the two, so I grasp onto the tub and move to get into it.

Raven moves by my side once more, holding my hand and letting me use him for balance.

"Is it hot enough for you?" he asks.

"Yes, it's perfect," I hum as he helps to lower me

into the tub while I hold my hair to keep it from getting wet. A moan leaves me at how heavenly the water and jets feel.

Raven stills behind me for a moment, then takes my hair and hangs it over the edge of the tub. "Is there anything I can get you?" he asks in a gruff voice.

"No." I take his hand and look up at him. "Thank you for this."

"Anything for you, my little star," he says, dropping a kiss on my forehead before settling in on the bench behind me.

Raven says those words so easily, yet they rip through me like a raging tide. I look around the bathroom to try and distract myself. The bathtub sits in the middle of an octagonal room with large windows surrounded by long black, gold, and silver drapery. The walls are made of wood, and wooden beams hang above me, as does a chandelier that would look beautiful lit up at night. There's a fireplace built into the wall on my right with a TV above it. The floors are made of the same silver marble as the countertops. It's expensive, opulent, and a place I never thought I'd be.

What am I doing here?

Everything suddenly crashes through me. The reality check I got earlier, the drug and near assault, that Raven likely murdered those two men but hasn't harmed me once.

Raven is holding the door open to everything I've ever wanted, and yet I'm terrified to trust him. If I reach out my hand to him, will he let me fall? Will he abandon or use me like everyone else in my life has? I want so badly to trust him, to listen to the feelings in my heart, but there's too much I need to know.

I take a deep breath to gather my courage before asking, "Raven...why did you save me last night? Why were you there?"

He tenses behind me. Then he pulls my hair onto his lap, his movements gentle as he curls strands between his fingers. His silence is weighted, like he's considering his words before he speaks.

"Truthfully, I wouldn't have been there, and that would have been the worst mistake of my life. I had not planned to go out at all, but then I grew restless. Nothing I did calmed me. I couldn't sit still, I couldn't quiet my mind. I took flight and then felt this undeniable pull, as if I was being led somewhere important. The moment I saw you, I knew you were what I was meant to find." His gaze softens as he looks at me.

I clasp my hands together under the water, trying to ignore the hopeful warmth that flows through me. "What was I doing when you found me?"

"Those *things*," he says the word with so much malice that a chill sweeps down my back, "had their hands on you. They drugged you, and you were nearly unconscious."

I lick my dry lips. "I didn't see you, not really, but I saw what you did to them."

Raven's face drops. "I apologize that you had to witness that."

"Why did you kill them, Raven? Are you normally that violent? Is that how you handle things?" I don't want him to say yes. I let those hands touch me. I'm letting him run those strong fingers through my hair right now, caress and soothe me, and I don't want any of it to end. I desperately want to understand, and I need him to help make it easier.

He sighs, but his eyes meet mine, and there is not a shred of doubt or shame in them. "There is so much I need to explain to you. Will you let me?"

"Yes," I say and brace myself for his story.

"I was created long ago, in an age when the world was still new and barely populated. We were tasked with guarding humans from dark forces who wished them harm."

"Dark forces?" The idea sounds incredible to me, but it's not like I ever thought I'd be sitting in a bathtub naked after fucking a man who has wings and a tail.

He nods. "Things like demons and other dark creatures exist. They tempt humans and eat away at their souls. After enough time, those humans turn into a darker version of themselves, monstrous but still human. They are cruel, violent, and will kill and infect everything they can, spreading the darkness like a disease. It was our duty—*is* my duty—to eradicate those creatures before they can damage the populace."

"You've gone through so much," I whisper. I try to

imagine if I could handle living Raven's life. The first humans were recorded over a million years ago. He's spent all that time seeing the darker sides of the world and having to save it with bloodshed. How is he still sane?

Raven picks up a Tangle Teezer, then takes a quarter of my long hair and begins to comb from the ends up to my scalp. The action and his gentleness surprise me. My gaze jumps to his face, but he isn't looking at me. Rather, he's staring intently at my hair, as if he needs the distraction. A part of me needs it too.

When he finishes, he sets the brush down. His voice is low, full of sadness, as he says, "It was difficult to see such heinous crimes. They were neverending. Many of my siblings fell to the darkness over time. They couldn't handle the battles, the creatures, or the loss of humans they tried to protect. I have done my best, but my soul has also been tainted by the darkness."

Raven picks up my hand and kisses it gently. "I have done horrible things, my little star, and at times— much like last night—I desired it and would have done more if you were not there. I was made for battle, for killing, to follow duty blindly. And for the time I've been alive, I have—mostly without question. But the moment I saw you, something changed. It was as if my soul recognized yours across time and space. I knew you were important. Destined to be mine."

Raven's hand slides to my cheek. "I understand that

this may all be new for you. It is new for me too. I understand that I may make mistakes. I don't know much about human etiquette, or even the name of emotions outside of fear and anger. But I want to learn. You have the most brilliant, radiant soul I have ever seen, and while I don't deserve you, I will try my hardest to. If you will teach me, I vow to spend eternity cherishing you."

He's so hopeful, putting his heart out on the line, and I want to take it, I do, but—

"Raven...I—I—there's so much you don't know about me. So much I've gotten wrong in my own life, and I'm scared. I want to trust you, I want to believe in whatever this is that's happening between us, but I'm terrified to make a mistake. To mess *this* up too."

Raven cups my head, and I wrap my hands around his large wrists. "Why are you so sure you will?"

"Because I always have!" I cry. "I've let people into my life who shouldn't be there, I've let people use me, allowed myself to be taken advantage of just because I was lonely. I was stupid and foolish and I have to do better, but that also means I need to heal. I need to see myself as someone worthy of more than that, but you shouldn't have to go through that with me."

"Cassandra," he croaks, and the way he says my name is too much. I turn my head away, but he grasps my chin, making me meet his eyes.

"My little star, my beautiful, incredible, little star,

do you think there's anywhere else I'd want to be than with you?"

Raven brushes his hand through my hair, sliding his fingers down the back of my neck. He holds it gently and caresses my ears with his thumbs. I can't turn away from him like this, can't argue, can't see anything but him. And as his eyes bore into mine, I know that's why he's done it. But I still can't answer him, because I want to believe him—my heart is screaming for me to—and yet I'm so enraptured by this man that I don't want to put him through all of that. It simply isn't fair.

He rubs my ears again, then strokes my neck with his fingers as he says, "I know about the Reddit post and what you went through last night. But it wasn't just that, was it? Tell me. Tell me all of it so I understand, and then you can see that I will still be here. That the choice I make will always be *you*."

My heart is in my throat, and I can do nothing more than nod. He wraps his arms around me, picks me up, and settles me onto his lap. He grabs a towel and begins to dry my back. When I shift to move away from him, not wanting to make him wet, he simply tightens his arm around my waist and shakes his head. So I stay and begin to tell him my story.

"My family was middle class," I start. "They wanted more for themselves. They were obsessed with it, and I think the only reason they had me was to try and further that goal."

Raven doesn't say anything, but his body grows taut. Still, his movements are gentle as he dries my arms and the tops of my thighs.

"As soon as I was born, they showed me off to everyone. One of my earliest memories is of them putting me against another child at our kindergarten graduation, sharing all the ways I was superior. I had to look the most elegant, enunciate my words the most accurately, never make a mistake, never look dirty, never complain or talk back. As I got older, they threw parties, places where I had to go mingle and make nice with the sons and daughters of anyone who had more money than us."

I take a deep breath, wishing I could ignore this part, somehow say it in a way that won't upset Raven. But I can't, so I simply tell the truth.

"My parents arranged a marriage between me and a boy from a more prominent family," I say. His chest begins to vibrate, his hand shaking as rage takes over his face. I rest my hand over his heart and quickly say, "It's okay, it didn't go through, and I'm sorry I had to tell you, but it's part of why—"

"It's alright," he says as he runs his hand over my back. "I understand, and I promised you I would listen. Tell me the rest."

I meet his eyes, see the certainty there, and force myself to swallow so I can speak again. "They wanted me to marry my father's boss's son, the next VP of the company. It would have secured enough money and status for a lifetime. But then my father found out my mother was having an affair with his boss, and she left. One day she was there, and the next she was gone. She didn't even say goodbye.

"My father couldn't handle it. He started drinking, doing drugs, and every day when he came home, he blamed me. For not being good enough, not doing enough. For not being perfect."

"Cassandra—" Raven says, but I cut him off.

"It's okay. I just...let me get through this," I whisper. At Raven's nod, I continue: "My father had two modes. He either neglected me or abused me; there was no in-between.

"I recognize that now, but at the time I just wondered, *Why me?* What did I do to upset him so much? Why couldn't I be what he wanted? Why couldn't I do more? Why was I such a bad daughter? But in the end, it didn't matter. None of it did," I shrug, "because my father, in his drunk, drug-induced haze, stole money and tried to hire someone to murder his boss, all to get revenge on him for sleeping with my mother. It didn't work, of course, but my father got caught and is in prison now. I had to change my name at eighteen so I wouldn't be involved or face any discrimination from the case. But that's why I—"

"Needed someone?" Raven asks.

"Yes. I just wanted to feel loved, to feel important. To have someone tell me that I didn't deserve every-

thing that I'd gone through, that I am enough for someone, that I deserve to be loved. To feel safe."

I'm shaking now. Raven holds me tighter and stares so deeply into my eyes that I feel like I'm drowning. Then he says the words I've always longed to hear: "You are important. You deserve to be loved, to feel safe. You are and have always been enough. I am so sorry that your parents didn't show that to you, that your friends didn't, but I will."

He wipes the tears from my eyes. "You don't have to believe me now. You don't even have to trust me. But I can say without question that I will show you. I would die for you, I will live for you, and if the feeling pounding through my heart right now is love, then know I will give it all to you. You are worth that, Cassandra. You are worth everything. Can you let me show that to you, my little star?"

My heart shatters into a million pieces. It feels as if he's the start to healing every wound I have, like he can fill every gap within me until I can't breathe without tasting his essence. He's in me, in my heart, my soul, and I don't want to ever lose that. I don't want to ever lose him.

"Yes," I cry. The word tumbles out once more before he claims my lips with his own.

6

CASSANDRA

To give this relationship a chance, I have to close out my old life. The first thing I need to do is contact my job so they don't think I've abandoned my position. When I explain this to Raven, he asks if I like working there.

"No, not really," I admit. "But I'm not quite ready to quit yet either." I have a strong need to depend solely on myself. Getting hired was hard enough, and if I ever have to find another job, it would be just as—if not more—difficult.

That hyper-independence is because of what I experienced in my childhood, and it's unhealthy. Until that fear subsides a little, though, I need to have some sort of fallback plan.

Raven nods in understanding. He calls Daniella—a woman he says we can trust—and within five minutes of explaining what we need, she sends over a doctor's note excusing me from work for three months.

I'm surprised but grateful for her help. I power on my phone to send it to my boss and find a flood of aggressive, abusive texts and voicemails from Chelsea, Amy, and Heather. They've filled my inbox to the brim with malice, saying I abandoned them at the bar.

They go on to tell me I deserve to be lying somewhere dead in a ditch, call me a bitch, an asshole, and every other name in the book. Not once do they even ask what happened to me—or why I disappeared.

Hurt and anger well up inside me until I cry from it all. Raven holds me close, caressing my back, being there for me in every way he can.

Once I've calmed down, he helps me craft a final message to the three of them. He encourages me to explain everything and hold nothing back. He believes that part of my misery is because I've never spoken up about my mistreatment. So I do.

I tell them how they ignored and used me last night, how they've hurt me for years, and that it all ends now. Then I wish them a nice life and block their numbers. And while I'm proud of myself for finally voicing my feelings, it'll take time to truly release the whole situation, especially the hurt, from my mind.

I email the doctor's note to my boss, not bothering to wait for a reply before shutting my phone off again.

Raven, despite all of his murderous glances toward the device, gives me a hug. "I know that was difficult for you, but you did what needed to be done," he says. "You showed so much courage, and I'm honored to be by your side, my little star."

His faith and support mean everything to me, and it's exactly what I need. But this is only the beginning. I need to work on myself. To be honest about the person I am and be willing to change the things that I don't like. I don't deserve Raven, but if I'm not willing to work on myself, I never will. I have to try and let go, to show the same courage Raven believes I have, that he inspires within me.

Because I do want this. I want him.

Raven spends the rest of the day trying to make me feel better, and the next day, and the next. And soon, we start to build a routine together.

My morning starts when I wake up naked and snuggled in Raven's arms. After we finally leave our bed, we take a shower. On wash day, Raven helps me detangle sections of my hair and apply product. He's even learned how to twist it just the way I like. Then he asks me if there's anything I would like to do that day.

Normally, I don't have anything in mind. I'm still not used to being able to have this freedom, to sleep and wake up when I want to, without having to think about work or meal plans.

I don't have to budget. Anything I want Raven gets me. In fact, I have to be careful whenever I do show interest in something, because he doesn't care what the price is. I mentioned once how nice his computer was, and he had a new one delivered to me within an hour.

He's observant with meals as well. I'm not a picky eater. There were times when I was younger that I was lucky to even get anything to eat at all. But every day, Raven asks what I want to eat.

At first, I tried to tell him anything was fine, but he would grimace and walk me around the kitchen, making me pick between different breads, cheeses, condiments, and proteins. Now, Raven keeps the kitchen stocked with my go-tos—bagels, brownies, fruits, cheeses, cold cuts, vegetables, my favorite snacks, and expensive chocolate that tastes divine.

After breakfast, Raven takes me on a tour of his castle. There are multiple floors, towers, and even a giant library, which he's gifted to me.

One day, he brings me to a large room full of windows, marble floors, and columns. Raven wraps his arm around my waist and pulls me flush against him, saying, "This used to be a ballroom. Perhaps, one day, when you get friends who are actually *worthy* of your time, we could throw a party for you here."

For a moment, I'm speechless. I open my mouth to tell Raven it's too much, that he doesn't have to do this for me, but he scratches the back of his neck and starts to blush. I can't say the words when he's like this, nervous that I'll say no. So I swallow hard, push the words back, and try for him.

He collects himself, then stares straight into my eyes.

"It would be for you," he whispers. *"Completely* for you. You'd have whatever you want. Whatever food you'd like, whatever music. We could even hire that band you enjoy. But it would all be for you. Everyone here would honor you like the queen you are. Everyone would *see* you. You wouldn't have to hide away. No one would make you uncomfortable, I promise you."

Tears well up in my eyes at his words. He seems to know my deepest, most hidden desires. How long have I wanted to be seen? To be cherished, surrounded by people who truly care about me? Not for what I can do for them or bring to them, but simply because I'm me, and I'm enough.

"Raven—" I croak and reach up to twine my arms around him.

He lifts me effortlessly, and I kiss him with every fiber in me, with every part of my heart that he's claimed. A fire sparks between us, and I want it to keep burning. I want this, him, forever. Not because of what he does for me or his kindness and generosity, but simply because of who he is.

I can't imagine not seeing his face one day, not hearing his laugh. I love how his nose scrunches when he's concentrating on something, the way he blushes and fidgets when he's shy, his warmth, even the sound of his footsteps or the flaps of his wings.

If I could, I'd go back in time. I'd fight harder to hold onto who I was, so I could be a better partner for him. I'd do everything I could to find him. I'd spend every second of my life with him so he'd never be alone. I'd make sure he experienced every type of happiness and joy. I would redo my whole life for him, I would relive my whole life for him.

He's my blessing, my guiding light. He deserves the world—and so help me, I'm going to give it to him.

"What would you like to do today?" Raven says as he wraps a towel around his waist.

My eyes roam over his body. If I hadn't spent so much time planning out today, I would have responded with, *"You."* But I restrain myself and say, "I'd like to go on a date."

Raven tilts his head and I giggle at his confusion.

He smiles and gives me a gentle kiss. "A date then. Is there anywhere specific you'd like to go?"

"Everything's already taken care of. We have an 8 p.m. reservation."

Raven raises an eyebrow. "Why do I feel like you're scheming something, little star?"

I giggle. "Because you know me far too well."

I PUT on the dress Fallon and I picked out and gasp at myself in the mirror. I told her I wanted something that would make me feel sexy, seductive, and powerful, and this dress does all of that and more. The sheer material wraps around my neck like a collar, leading to the black sweetheart neckline that hugs my breasts perfectly. The dress flows down to my ankles, with two slits running all the way up my thighs. And I know I made the right decision the moment Raven looks at me with a glint in his eye.

He pulls me into his arms, but I put my finger on his lips right before he kisses me. "No. We have a reservation."

"It can wait," he says, bending to kiss me again.

I pull back from him. "Dinner first. You can take this off afterward."

He pouts playfully, even as his tail thumps behind him in joy.

Dinner is incredible, but nothing is better than Raven's company. I would have never thought my life would end up this way, that I could be so happy, feel so cherished. I hoped for it for so long, and now that I have this love, I'll never let it go. Raven's mine and I'm his, and tonight I will show him that.

When Raven pulls into the long private road to our home, I put my hand on his knee. "Stop here."

"Why?"

"Please, there's something I want to give you."

Raven watches me for a moment, then puts the car

in park. I open my door and he follows me to the front of the car.

"Do you know what primal play is?" I ask him, clasping my hands hard to try and steady myself.

"No." Raven takes my hands and kisses each finger, and I know he can sense my nervousness.

"It's a sexual activity. You would be the hunter, and I would be your prey."

The words are barely out of my mouth when Raven's eyes flash to a color I've never seen before, a bright, glowing white. It's so quick that I almost think I've imagined it, until he growls, "Cassandra—"

"Chase me," I whisper. "Chase me. Hunt me. I want you to. You always hold back. You're always so worried about hurting me, but you won't, even if you lose control." I cup his cheek, caress his skin, and he nuzzles my hand.

The look on his face is a mixture of excitement and trepidation, and it makes me love him even more.

"I trust you," I say. We rest our foreheads against one another's, share the air we breathe, and then I take a single step backward, then another, and another.

He looks tormented, and I say it again, trying to convince him: "I trust you. I *love* you."

His eyes widen at the confession, and it only makes my smile grow.

"Now count to ten and come find me, if you can." I smirk.

His nostrils flare and his pupils dilate at the challenge. And before he says the number "one," I'm off.

"Two," he says out loud.

I dash into the forest.

"Three," his voice booms.

I keep running.

"Four."

My heart is pounding in my chest from a mixture of fear and excitement, and the thought of what he'll do when he catches me makes me more wet than I've ever been.

"Five."

I kick off my shoes, throw them in different directions to try and trick him. I keep running, step on the sharp end of a rock, and the sudden pain makes me tumble onto the forest floor.

"Six."

I don't have time to lie there. I get back up, using all of my adrenaline to run farther away from his voice.

"Seven."

Panic rushes through me at how soon he'll set out to find me, and he *will* find me. I run farther through the densest part of the forest, thinking that will keep him from searching for me from above. There's a small river that runs through here, and if I can just cross it—

"Eight." His voice is right in my ear, and I scream.

It turns into a shriek as he turns me around and propels us into the air, above the canopy, making my eardrums pop. My fight-or-flight response kicks in, and I try to pull away from him.

Raven doesn't budge. If anything, his arms grip me tighter, and before I can even process that we're floating in the sky, his lips slam against mine. I push on his chest, and he pulls me closer. I bite his lip, and he growls and slaps my ass hard. The sharp sting shocks me for just a moment, and it's all he needs before his mouth is on me again.

He kisses me like he needs to devour me, to brand me as his. It's a mixture of lips, tongues, and teeth, and I love it. I love how enlarged his fangs are, how they scrape against my lips when he bites me. He steals my every breath, and he can have them all. He can take whatever he wants. Every part of me.

I raise my hands to grab onto him, but he uses his tail to tie them behind my back. I wiggle and writhe against him, but he still won't let me go. I'm exhilarated by the danger of him, and I want him so badly it hurts. I need him, *right* now.

"Raven," I whimper in between his harsh kisses.

He pulls back just enough for me to finally look at him.

I gasp.

His white skin is now dark gray. It looks thicker around his bulging muscles, like armor, yet smooth like stone. His face is all sharp, hard angles. And his eyes—the deepest darkest black, with luminescent white irises. He's a perfect contradiction, like a beast stuck in mid-transformation: not quite human and not quite animal, but a mixture of the strongest parts of both.

He's breathtakingly beautiful, and perhaps the most incredible part of this is the knowledge that he is completely and entirely *mine*.

Raven must see something in me because he suddenly releases my wrists and loops his tail around my waist and hips. I wrap my arms around him, pushing my body against his. I let out a frustrated groan at the clothes separating us. Raven understands immediately and shreds the material until it flutters around us in tiny pieces.

The air is cold, but the feeling of Raven's hot skin against mine only stokes the fire in me higher. I wrap my legs around his hips, and for a moment we stare into each other's eyes, panting. I don't need to clarify what I want. He knows.

I don't need foreplay. I don't need anything but the connection we've built between one another and his cock deep in my pussy.

And he gives it to me. Raven thrusts so deep inside of me it robs the air from my lungs.

He fucks me like an animal. He's hard, fast, out of control, and the only thing I can do is surrender to him. He wraps my hair around his wrist until he gets to the scalp and pulls my head back, the perfect amount of pain.

He's making me submit to him, punishing me for

our play, and it only makes me hotter. He can punish me for as long and hard as he wants—and he does. My body is nothing more than a toy to play with, something for him to sink into. And that's exactly what I need. He bites my neck, his fangs sinking into my skin, and I scream.

He fucks me harder, faster, until all I can feel is him. The world fades away, and he's my singular purpose. I hold onto him for dear life, crying out his name as he keeps ramming into me. Then I'm coming, jerking, writhing, trembling against him. And he keeps going. It's like his hips are moving of their own accord. He tosses his head back and roars as he comes inside of me. It's an incredibly beautiful sight, and I moan at the feeling of him spilling in me.

For a moment, we're simply floating there, but when his knot releases, he slips out of me and brings us back down to the hard ground.

"Get on all fours," he demands, and my eyes widen. "I'm not done with you yet."

I get on my hands and knees. At first he doesn't move. I turn my head and see him staring at me, his eyes a mixture of awe and desire, as if he's memorizing my every curve.

He sinks to his knees behind me and says, "If it hurts, tell me to stop." And then he thrusts inside of me once more, filling me to the brim.

He grabs my hips, pushing me back on his cock, fucking me harder, deeper. He's brutal, untamed, and it drives me crazy. Raven puts his hand in my hair and pushes on my head until my chest is on the ground. Then he growls, squats behind me, and rams back inside of me over and over again. I grab onto the dirt, sticks, leaves. A twig scrapes against my chest, and I don't care as long as Raven doesn't stop.

"Is this what you wanted?" he snarls.

"Yes, *yes*! Oh God, Oh God, Oh *God*—"

Raven wraps his hand around my neck and pulls me back against his chest. "If you're going to scream anyone's name, it will be mine and *only* mine." His voice is dark, threatening, but it only makes my pussy clench around him.

"Raven—"

He thrusts inside me once more. "That's my good girl. Now take your monster's cock and come all over it."

I'm lost to him. I know nothing but this. He turns his head and kisses me. He licks my mouth, rubs his tongue against mine, all while he chokes me. I grab onto his thighs and force my legs wider to take him deeper. And then I come so hard that stars shine behind my eyes, and he follows me into the abyss.

EPILOGUE
CASSANDRA

Two lines. It's positive. I'm pregnant.

I shouldn't be surprised. For weeks Raven's been telling me that I smell different. He's noticed little changes in me, and it's not like we've ever used protection. But having this test in my hand makes it a reality.

I refuse to tell him yet, though. These tests can be false positives, and it'll be difficult to get another one to confirm. Raven was already suspicious when I told him I wanted to go to the store without him. Trying that again won't work, so I do the only thing I can—I call Daniella. We've met multiple times, and she's always been willing to help.. The moment I explain to her what I need, she gets me an appointment for that afternoon. Then all that's left to do is tell Raven.

When I tell Raven I want to meet up with Daniella at first, he's fine. But the moment I clarify that I need to meet her alone, his face falls, and no matter what I do or how many times I ask him to tell me what's wrong, he won't. So, I simply cup his face and remind him that I love him, and even though he says the words back to me, he's still not okay.

Soon I have to go, and when I arrive at the Agency's facilities, I swear I see Raven's dark wings peeking out from behind a tree. I chuckle at how thoughtful and silly he is, and it's the perfect thing to ease my nerves.

An hour later, it's confirmed. I'm pregnant. They're even able to use magic to tell me the gender—a little baby boy. They assure me that he's healthy. Since he's not one hundred percent human, there are certain diseases and concerns we won't ever have to face. That relieves me, but also opens up a million other questions.

What about me? I'm human, Raven isn't. He has wings, and I don't think my uterus is built for that. But they explain that while I am still human, being with Raven has extended my lifespan to match his, so there's no risk of death. Additionally, most creatures don't develop protrusions like wings until after they're born.

I leave the appointment in shock. It's so much to take in, and when I see Raven sitting on a bench in the lobby, it feels like it's a little easier to breathe under the weight of it all.

That is, until I see him staring down at his hands with the saddest expression I've ever seen.

I immediately reach for him and cup his face in my hands. "Raven? What's wrong?"

"Are you leaving me? Did I do something wrong?"

I shake my head, confused. "No, you make me the happiest I've ever been. Why would you think that?"

"You wanted to meet with Daniella alone. I thought maybe you wanted her help to leave and—"

"Baby, no! No," I say with a gentle but firm tone. "I love you, I'm *in* love with you."

"Then why—"

I take his hands in mine and put them on my stomach. "Because we're having a baby."

His eyes grow so wide that if he hadn't been upset a second ago, I would laugh.

"I wanted to make sure before I told you, so I needed to meet with a doctor and confirm."

He blinks rapidly, and his face is filled with such surprise and awe that I can't help but smile.

"We're... There's a baby in there? Our baby?" He rubs my stomach and I nod.

"Mmhmm, a little boy."

"A boy..." he says in disbelief. Then he stands and lifts me in the air. "A boy! We're having a baby!"

I laugh as he spins me around and kisses me until I'm breathless.

"Are you alright? Are you healthy? What do you need? What should I get you? Are you hungry?"

I laugh then, so hard that tears come out of my

eyes. Raven sets me on my feet and gently wipes at them, all while keeping one arm around me.

"The only thing I want is to go home with you."

"Then we'll go home." He kisses my head with a blissful smile on his lips. "I love you," he whispers into my hair.

"I love you too."

The End of My Brutal Beast.

Want to read about a mafia queen who doesn't need anyone and the mafia king who will kill to stand by her side? Scan the QR code below!

Don't forget to join my newsletter to get a bonus scene of Mya's song, all the latest updates, ARC opportunities, and more!

ABOUT THE AUTHOR

Melissa had a difficult time speaking as a child, and thus writing became her best friend. There she learned the power of emotion, how to communicate heartbreak, sadness, tragedy, and still hope for something better: the happy ever after.

She loves to write imperfect, possessive heroes, that will risk their lives for those they love, strong heroines that can hold their own, and steamy scenes that grab you by the throat and bring you to your knees.

Melissa lives in a small town off the coast of Egypt, and is a huge mythology buff, with a love of all things magical, supernatural, paranormal, and steeped in lore and fantasy. When she is not writing Melissa can be found singing and dancing her heart out, or up, late at night, contemplating space and the universe with a large cup of tea.

facebook.com/MelissaCumminsAuthor

instagram.com/melissacumminsauthor

bookbub.com/profile/melissa-cummins

ACKNOWLEDGMENTS

Clare and Hannah, thank you both for your valuable feedback and making things easy so I can stay sane.

To you. Yes! You! Thank you so much for reading my novel. Knowing that you took the the time to read it is beyond amazing to me. You help every author to move forward, to write their next book, to publish, to celebrate. That's all you. So thank you again, take care, and I can't wait for you to read my next book!